TELL ME MORE! science

Creepy Crawly
SLIME MOLDS

by Ruth Owen

Ruby Tuesday Books

Published in 2021 by Ruby Tuesday Books Ltd.

Designer: Emma Randall
Editor: Mark J. Sachner
Production: John Lingham

Photo credits:
Alamy: 13; FLPA: 5 (top); Nature Picture Library: 14–15, 16;
Ruby Tuesday Books: 20; Science Photo Library: 4 (bottom), 17, 18–19, 21;
Shutterstock: Cover, 1, 4 (top), 5 (bottom), 6–7, 8–9, 10–11, 12, 22–23.

Library of Congress Control Number: 2020946808
Print (hardback) ISBN 978-1-78856-174-7
Print (paperback) ISBN 978-1-78856-175-4
eBook ISBN 978-1-78856-176-1

Printed and published in the United States of America
For further information including rights and permissions requests,
please contact: **shan@rubytuesdaybooks.com**

Contents

Let's Talk Slime!

We've all heard of slime. You may have played with slime or even made some.

Your nose produces about 2 pints of thick slime every day!

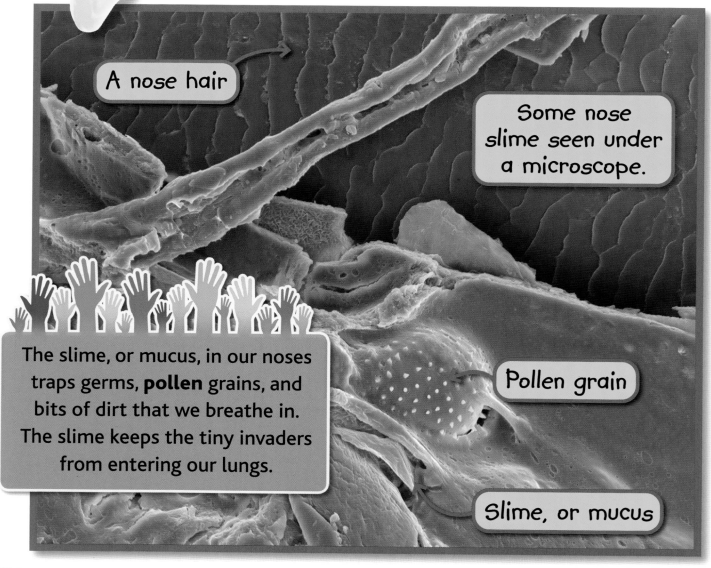

A nose hair

Some nose slime seen under a microscope.

The slime, or mucus, in our noses traps germs, **pollen** grains, and bits of dirt that we breathe in. The slime keeps the tiny invaders from entering our lungs.

Pollen grain

Slime, or mucus

Slugs are covered with sticky slime that helps them slide over the ground.

Slug slime

But did you know that there is actually a kind of slime that's alive?

It's called slime **mold**.

Slime mold

What Is Slime Mold?

Slime molds live in gardens, parks, and forests all over the world.

They ooze over rotting leaves and logs.

Scientists used to think that these slimy living things were a type of mold, or **fungi**.

That's how they got their name.

A slime mold
on a rotting log

Now scientists say that slime molds belong to a group of living things called myxomycetes (mik-soh-MAHY-seetz).

Slime molds live where it is dark, damp, and cool. This keeps them soft and jello-like and stops them from drying out.

Weird and Wonderful

There are about **900** different types of slime molds.

They come in many different shapes and colors, except for green.

1

Slime molds are never green because they don't contain chlorophyll (KLAWR-uh-fil). Chlorophyll is the substance that makes plants green.

Each type of slime mold has a long science name.

2

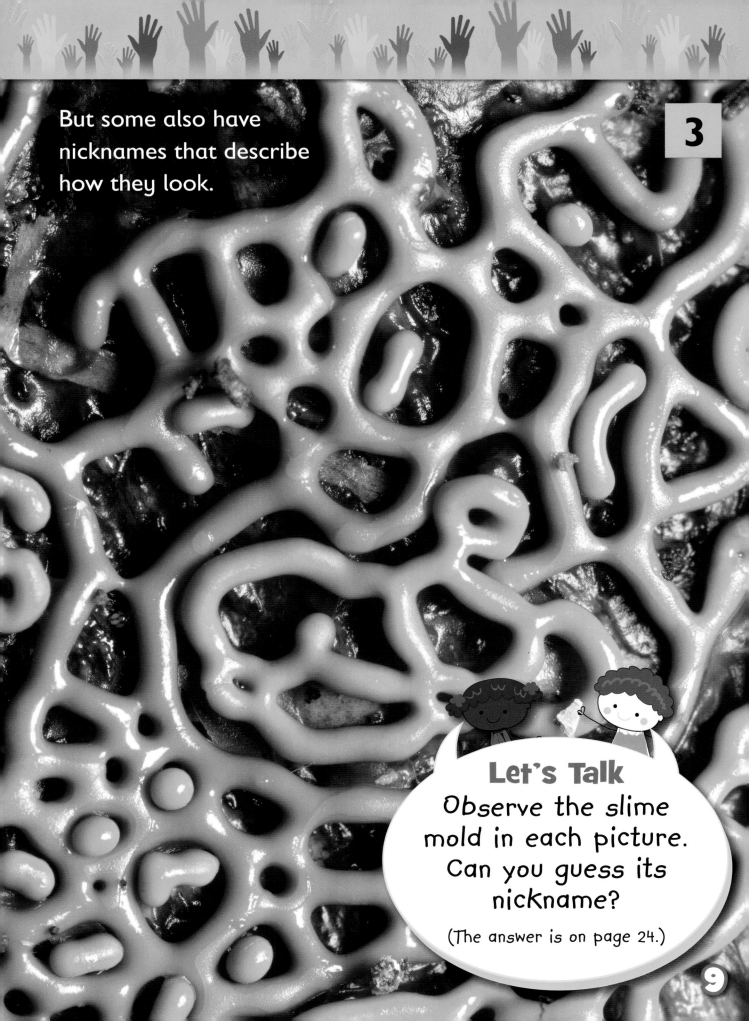

But some also have nicknames that describe how they look.

Let's Talk

Observe the slime mold in each picture. Can you guess its nickname?

(The answer is on page 24.)

Hungry Slime

How does a slime mold with no mouth and no stomach feed?

To find food, a slime mold sends out branch-like **tendrils**.

Fungus

Slime mold feeding on a fungus

Once it finds a meal, the slime mold crawls over the food and completely covers it.

Next, the slime mold releases special substances that break down the food.

Finally, the blob of slime mold soaks up **nutrients** from its food.

Let's Talk
Slime molds are very helpful to forests and gardens. Why?

(The answer is on page 24.)

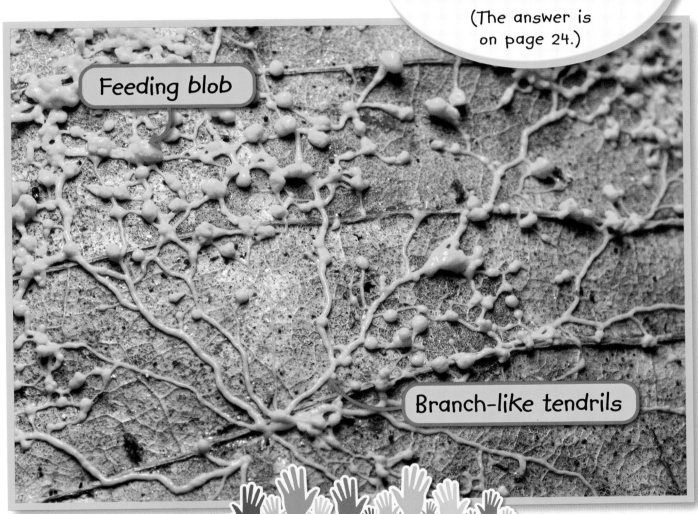

Feeding blob

Branch-like tendrils

Slime molds feed on fungi and **bacteria** that grow on rotting wood and dead leaves.

A Slime Mold Goes Hunting

Once a slime mold tendril finds food, it sends a message through the rest of the slime.

Then other tendrils ooze to the spot where the food has been found.

To test this, scientists put some food and a slime mold into a maze.

The slime mold's tendrils searched the maze's passages.

Once a tendril found food, it sent out a message.

Then other tendrils changed direction and found their way through the maze to the food!

Maze

This slime mold is being tested by a scientist.

Oats

This tendril has found the food.

The slime mold in this picture can move at about half an inch (1.25 cm) per hour.

Tendrils searching for food

Slime Mold Survival

If a slime mold cannot find enough food, a big change happens.

The slime grows tiny blobs on stalks called fruiting bodies.

Tiny fruiting body

Slime mold fruiting bodies are so small that dozens of them would fit on the tip of a pencil.

Tip of a pencil

Inside each fruiting body there are millions of **spores**.

A spore is a little like a seed.

Let's Talk
What happens to a slime mold if the weather gets too dry?

(The answer is on page 24.)

Making More Slime

A fruiting body bursts open and its spores are released.

Inside each **microscopic** spore is everything that's needed to make a new slime mold.

Spores and threads

Fruiting bodies

The pictures on these pages were taken with a powerful microscope.

There are microscopic threads inside a fruiting body that wriggle in the air. This helps propel, or flick, the spores away from the fruiting body.

Thread

Slime mold spores

Once a slime mold has produced spores, it turns black and dies.

A Tiny New Slime Mold

Each tiny spore from the fruiting bodies becomes a slime mold.

The microscopic new slime mold is called an **amoeba** (uh-MEE-buh).

Animals and people are made of billions of tiny parts called **cells**.

A slime mold amoeba is made of just one cell.

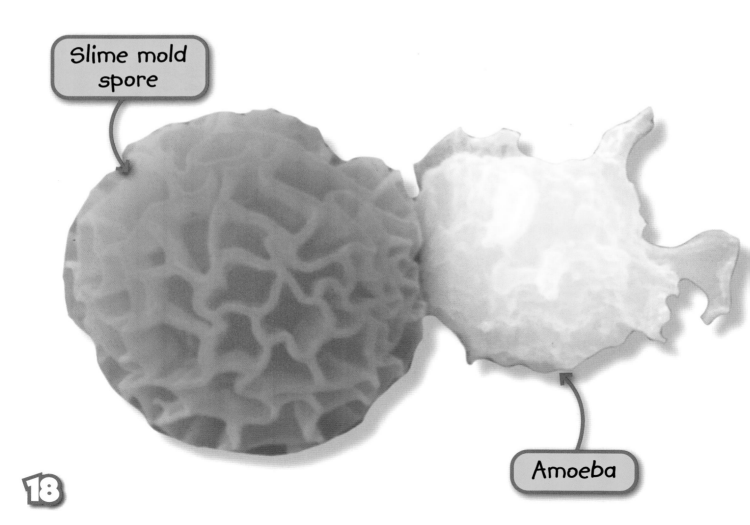

Slime mold spore

Amoeba

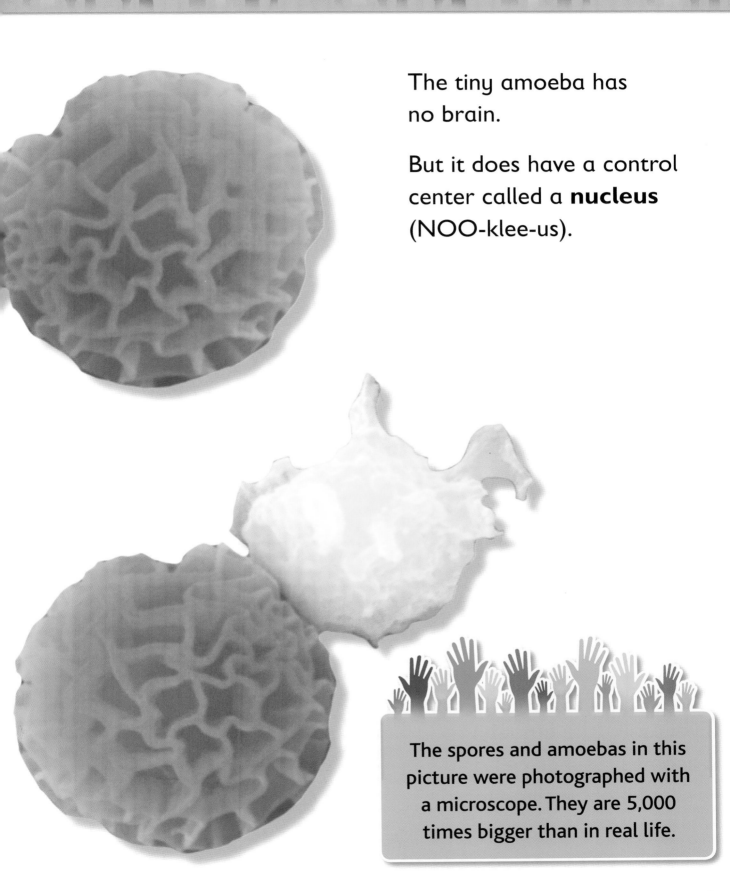

The tiny amoeba has no brain.

But it does have a control center called a **nucleus** (NOO-klee-us).

The spores and amoebas in this picture were photographed with a microscope. They are 5,000 times bigger than in real life.

Dividing and Growing

A slime mold amoeba may be tiny, but it has a way of growing bigger.

If an amoeba finds lots of food, its nucleus, or control center, divides into two.

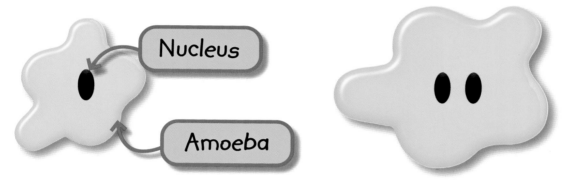

Nucleus

Amoeba

This allows the single cell amoeba to grow.

Each nucleus in the cell divides again and again.

Eventually, the amoeba becomes a super cell or a slimy blob of slime mold.

Super cell

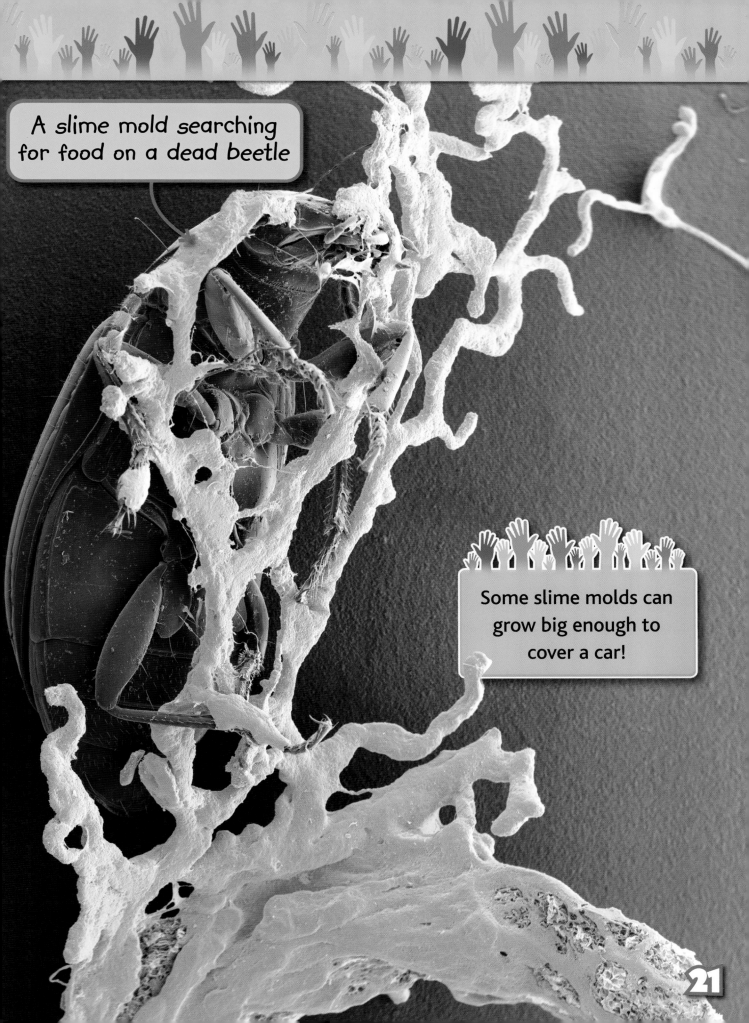

A slime mold searching for food on a dead beetle

Some slime molds can grow big enough to cover a car!

Be a Slime Mold Investigator

Imagine you are a scientist who has discovered some slime mold in a forest. You must take a photo of your discovery or draw it. Then write a short report about this fascinating living thing. (But first, you must make some gooey slime!)

Gather Your Equipment:

- Some dead leaves and twigs
- A bowl
- ½ tablespoon baking soda
- 4 fluid ounces (114 ml) white glue
- A spoon
- Yellow food coloring
- 1 tablespoon contact lens solution
- A camera or cell phone
- A notebook and pens or pencils

7 Finally, write a short report about slime molds that includes your top 5 favorite facts about this living slime.

1 Mix together the baking soda and white glue in the bowl.

2 Add five drops of yellow food coloring to the bowl and mix well. If you want the color to be stronger, add more drops little by little, stirring the mixture well.

3 Add the contact lens solution to the bowl. Now keep stirring until the mixture turns to slime.

4 Lift the slime from the bowl and knead and squish it with your hands until the slime is fully formed.

5 Lay out your leaves and twigs and then spread your slime over them. Try making tendrils that are searching for food.

6 Take a photo of your slime mold model, print it out, and then glue it into your notebook. If you prefer, you can draw your slime mold.

Let's Talk
How are slime molds similar to and different from plants?

(There are some answers on page 24.)

Glossary

amoeba
A living thing made up of just one cell.

bacteria
Microscopic living things. Some bacteria are helpful, while others, known as germs, can cause disease.

cell
A very tiny part of a plant, animal, human, or other living thing.

fungi
A group of living things that include mushrooms, toadstools, and mold.

microscopic
So tiny it can only be seen through a microscope.

mold
A type of soft, crumbly fungus that grows and feeds on materials such as old food or dead leaves.

nucleus
The part of a cell that works as the cell's control center.

nutrients
Substances that are needed by living things to help them grow and stay healthy.

pollen
Dust-like grains made by flowers that plants need for making seeds.

spore
A tiny part of a slime mold that contains everything needed to grow a new slime mold. Spores act a little like a plant's seeds.

tendril
A long, thin, thread-like part of a slime mold or plant.

Wolf's milk slime mold

Index

Read More

Lawrence, Ellen. *Creeping Slime
(Slime-Inators & Other Slippery Tricksters).*
Minneapolis, MN: Bearport Publishing
(2019).

Owen, Ruth. *Welcome to the Forest
(Nature's Neighborhoods: All About Ecosystems).*
Minneapolis, MN: Ruby Tuesday Books (2016).

Answers

Pages 8-9:
1) Dog vomit slime mold
2) Scrambled egg slime mold
3) Pretzel slime mold

Page 11:
As a slime mold feeds on fungi and bacteria, it helps break down dead leaves and wood. Slime molds are part of nature's clean-up crew because they keep gardens and forests free of rotting, dead plants.

Page 15:
If the weather gets too dry, a slime mold becomes a crusty, hard lump called a sclerotium (skli-ROH-shee-uhm). It can live like this for years! When it rains, the lump soaks up water and becomes jello-like again.

Page 22:
Both slime molds and plants live in gardens and forests. Slime molds can move from place to place, but plants grow in one spot. Slime molds move around to find food. Then they soak up nutrients from their food. Plants make their own food using sunlight, water, and carbon dioxide from the air. They also take in nutrient from the soil with their roots. Both slime molds and plants can produce more of themselves. Slime molds produce fruiting bodies that contain spores. Most plants produce seeds in flowers and fruits.